Last Girl In

Kerry-Ann fights
to stay in the game

Cheryl Diane Parkinson

Edited by Sonya McGilchrist

DINOSAUR
BOOKS

www.dinosaurbooks.co.uk

All Rights Reserved
Published by Dinosaur Books Ltd, London
The rights of Cheryl Diane Parkinson to be identified as the
author of this work has been asserted by her in
accordance with the
Copyright, Designs and Patents Act, 1988

ISBN 978-1-9993363-7-0

British Library Cataloguing in Publication Data
A CIP catalogue record for this book is available from the
British Library.

For my dad, Andsurd Parkinson, who loved everything cricket and was a firm fan of the WINDIES.

Cheryl Diane Parkinson

CHAPTER ONE

Kerry-Ann slid open the window and breathed in the crisp morning air.

The street was empty.

She eased out onto the ledge, one hand securing her position and the other pushing her glasses further up her nose. Her leg curled round the drainpipe, and she slid to the ground.

"Kerry-Ann! Are you hearing me girl?"

Mum's voice reached her from inside the house – but there was no *way* – she wasn't gonna stop…

She was out of there!

Smiling triumphantly, she tiptoed around Mum's best rose bush and then ran as quickly as she could, disappearing down the street.

A minute later she came to a road lined with stalls selling just about everything – clothes, furniture, fruit and veg – if you could think of it, there was someone here selling it, for sure.

The street market was noisy, crowded and buzzing with life.

Kerry-Ann loved it.

The air around her was sweetened with the aromas of cooking food, fresh pastries, ripe fruit – and it was alive with music blasting from the stalls. Bob Marley's voice reached her, wrapping her in the warmth of the Caribbean.

She strolled, hands in her pockets.

"Marnin' Miss Kerry-Ann!"

It was Mrs Goody, a friendly, older woman who – for as long as Kerry-Ann could remember – had made it her business to keep an eye on her.

Kerry-Ann waved, side-stepping a cheerful dreadlocked man as she continued down the street, humming along to Bob Marley as she went. The music made her feel great...

Mrs Goody looked over from her stall, which was stacked with bags, scarves and jumpers, and smiled as she watched her go.

Ten minutes later, Kerry-Ann was walking out onto a wide open space – a fresh, green cricket field.

The sun broke through the clouds and, in her mind, Kerry-Ann filled the empty ground with spectators until there was not a single space free.

She strode past the pavilion and heard the imaginary crowds chatter as she approached the pitch. She could hear the commentator in her mind too:

Kerry-Ann Taylor. Fairly new to the game. Talented player, coming up to the crease. The whole game rests on what she does now. The pressure must be unbelievable!

Kerry-Ann smiled and waved, acknowledging the fans. She heard a ripple of excited chatter. They had all come here for one reason: to see the girl who was fast becoming a legend, the next Ebony Rainford-Brent…

Prepare to see history in the making here today… the commentator continued.

The crowd fell still. Kerry-Ann took a middle stump guard then checked her stance. The bowler began their run up and she readied herself for the ball that would come flying at her any moment now, her lips making a narrow, stubborn line inside her helmet. Everyone was watching.

And then her daydream evaporated.

"Hey!"

It was Amardeep, her best friend.

Kerry-Ann grinned at him, back in the real world.

"All right?"

"Yeah," he nodded. "Brought my new ball," and he tossed it into the air, displaying it proudly. "It's a Dukes."

Kerry raised her eyebrows.

"Nice. Where'd you get it?"

"My dad. Thought we could try it out?"

"Oh yes!"

Kerry-Ann took the ball and sniffed it. It still had that new ball smell.

"Did you know," she said, "that the first cricket ball was made of wool?"

'Did you know' was one of their private games – a running joke between them. They'd been doing it for so long that Kerry-Ann had forgotten how it started.

"No way!" gasped Armadeep. "No *way*!" – although of course he did know, and she *knew* that he knew, and he *knew* that she knew that…

"Yeah," she continued. "Shepherds made the game up to pass the time while guarding their sheep."

"Well…did you know that a cricket ball must weigh 163 grams exactly? *Exactly.*"

"No way," she gasped. "No *way!*" – although she had told him this very fact the day before.

"Amazing…"

But now Amardeep was looking over her shoulder. And his smile had vanished.

"Uh oh," he muttered. "There's a Moose on the loose."

****

Monty Marchmont – known as Moose – was striding towards them. And there could be no doubt about what he was planning to do. Dressed head to toe in pristine white training gear with a matching cap, he looked as formal and neat as a Test match opener.

Behind him strolled Jack, equally smart, a bat

under his arm. Kerry-Ann glanced down, taking in his cricket shoes – brand new and expensive – then looked up to see him grinning at her.

"What are you two doing here?" Moose said, his face an exaggerated frown. "Some mistake?"

"Er.. it's the cricket club, what do you think?" said Kerry-Ann.

She tossed Amardeep's new ball up and down.

"Really?" laughed Jack. "A cricket club! You think you're so smart – but sorry to disappoint you."

"We're not disappointed," Amardeep chipped in. "And she is smart. Smarter than you. We got here first, so *we* get to use the field. That's the rule."

Moose sighed and shook his head.

"Not any more. Didn't you check the *new* rota?"

Then – as if he'd forgotten they even existed – he turned and waved at a group of boys who were heading across the field towards them.

Kerry-Ann counted. There were eight of them, all older than her, and all laughing and striding forwards.

Moose was captain of the Under 15s First XI

and it looked as though most of his team had turned up for a practise session. Kerry-Ann and Amardeep were in the mixed Under 14s and knew the older boys by sight only.

From the corner of her eye she saw Amardeep crossing his arms, preparing to stand his ground.

"John, Leo, good to see you…"

Moose was shaking their hands warmly.

"…Harry, Josh, glad you could make it. Anyone seen Theo?"

"We're not going anywhere," Amardeep said stubbornly. "You lot can wait till we're done."

Moose raised an eyebrow.

"You don't have a choice. We've booked the ground. Nets too. Go and look if you don't believe me."

Kerry-Ann was aware of the others staring at them, amused. The older boys closed in around them.

"Come on team, we've got practise to do…"

Moose glanced back at Kerry-Ann and Amardeep with a satisfied smile, as he and his teammates sauntered off.

Kerry-Ann frowned and folded her arms in defiance. But it was no use.

Moose had won, and they all knew it.

CHAPTER TWO

Kerry-Ann lay on her bed, gazing up at the ceiling.

Moose had got in the way of practise. *Again!*

This was becoming a habit. And it was infuriating – he was so entitled.

She rolled onto her side. What did he have against her anyway – was it that she was a girl? Or because she was younger than him?

He just seemed to get in her way, all the time.

She rolled back over.

Maybe there was another reason though…a reason why he was always blocking her…

No! That was ages ago. I can't be held responsible. I was only a kid…

A feeling of guilt bubbled up briefly, but she pushed it down again, refusing to let it in, forcing herself to focus on the present.

She needed a solution. And she needed it now.

This situation with Moose was getting in the way of her cricket.

Playing cricket…that's what mattered.

After Moose had kicked them off the field, Kerry-Ann had retreated to the pavilion and checked the rota.

Amardeep hovered as she speed-read the new printed sheet – *Amended Rules and Regulations* – pinned to the green felt noticeboard.

She groaned.

"He's right. He has it booked. All of it."

She'd flipped out her phone. She needed to tell their teammates not to bother coming down.

Sorry everyone – need to reschedule.

"That's not fair!" Amardeep thumped his fist against the wall.

Kerry-Ann was squinting at the paper, trying to make sense of the small print – *Rules for Booking.*

So now, practise sessions could be booked in advance! But only in person, and only 24 hours before play. How was that gonna work? She was at school five days a week.

There wouldn't be enough time to race over.
Unless she skipped lunch maybe? But even then…

How had Moose managed it? He must have
someone to book up the slots for him…His mum,
maybe?

"There's got to be something we can do,"
Amardeep was saying.

"Could your mum book for us?" asked
Kerry-Ann.

"Nope. Working. Yours?"

"Same."

Amardeep had turned back to face the field.
The sun was shining merrily on Moose and his
mates and the ground echoed with their shouts and
laughter.

Kerry-Ann could see Amardeep's thoughts
skating across his face.

She knew that part of him wanted to go out
there, sit on the bench and watch the older boys
practise.

She sighed and they both watched as Jack
prepared himself for the next ball.

He stood sideways, his feet comfortably apart. Amardeep took a step towards the door so he could watch more closely.

Jack's head was totally still, focused on the bowler. He knew what he was doing. Anticipating what kind of ball would come his way and how to handle it. The bowler moved backwards, then began his run-up.

Jack turned from his previous side-on position to face the bowler straight on. Amardeep grinned as he realised Jack's plan.

The ball shot towards Jack, fast. As it bounced upwards, he shifted his weight to his right foot, bent his right leg and, lifting his bat in front of him, he effortlessly tapped the ball over his left shoulder.

The ball soared right over the wicket keeper to the boundary.

A beautiful scoop shot. Amardeep huffed begrudgingly.

Kerry-Ann glared.

She hated that these boys had taken their space. She hated that she'd blown-out her friends – in her pocket, she could feel her phone buzzing with replies – but also, she had to admit it, even if she would never utter the words aloud, Jack was good.

Kerry-Ann echoed Amardeep's huff.

"Come on…" she said, and they had turned and left.

CHAPTER THREE

The bedside clock was bleeping.

7.02 am.

Which meant…

"Kerry-Ann? Time to get up!" Mum pushed her way into Kerry-Ann's room – drawing her curtains, opening her wardrobe – and began shifting noisily through the clothes. The hangers clanged, reverberating in Kerry-Ann's ears.

It was Sunday. Which meant church.

"Mum?" she croaked, reaching for her glasses on the chest of drawers beside her bed. She fumbled them on and waited for the blur that was her Mum to become clear.

"You need to get ready." Mum pulled out a dress – the yellow one – and laid it on the chair.

"Here you go."

Too tired to argue, Kerry-Ann screwed her eyes shut and pulled the bed sheet over her head. This was the last thing she needed.

"Come on downstairs so I can do your hair. Your cereal's ready."

Moments later, Kerry-Ann peeled herself out of bed and, still in her pyjamas, made her way to the living room. Mum was watching Sunday morning television. Light streamed in through the windows. Mum had her new white blinds turned up, their shiny slats angled to let the sun in. She had seen them in one of those home decor articles she liked to read.

Kerry-Ann peered outside.

On the window ledge, two yellow eyes stared back. The cat yawned. Kerry-Ann yawned too. Lazily, the cat turned its attention away from her and started bathing itself.

Mum motioned for Kerry-Ann to sit on the floor between her legs. Coconut oil in her lap, she began meticulously parting Kerry-Ann's hair and smoothing in the oil.

"We're going to pick up Nana this morning. Grandpa's still not feeling well."

Kerry-Ann shovelled cornflakes into her mouth.

"It's been ages since we all went to church," Mum continued. "I can't remember the last time we went with Nana, can you? It will be nice."

Kerry Ann crunched. It was not that she hated church. She didn't. It was boring, but she believed in God and all that, and so she didn't have any major objections except the droning on of the priest all the time.

No, what she objected to most was the early morning.

Mass was something ridiculous, like 9.30 am. Which meant picking up Nana by 8.30 am. Which meant leaving by 8.00 am. Which meant Mum got Kerry-Ann up by 7.00 am. On a weekend!

There had to be a law against that kind of stuff. She was pretty sure that Jesus himself would object, if he had to wake up at that hour on a Sunday after getting up early all week for school.

She finished off the cornflakes, and pushed her glasses up her nose. Mum massaged her scalp a little, rubbing in the oil carefully before teasing the hair with a comb.

Occasionally the comb snagged and Kerry-Ann winced, but Mum pretended not to notice as she parted the hair in two and began cornrowing it neatly.

Kerry-Ann ignored the tugging at her scalp. She needed to focus on more important matters.

She needed to fight back.

She needed to out-think Moose. To find a way round him block-booking the pitch and nets.

"Go on and get ready now," Mum was saying. "We need to leave in half an hour."

****

The pew was cold and hard.

O Lord my God,
When I in awesome wonder
Consider all the works
Thy hand hath made

Nana was singing. Her eyes were looking up towards the church roof. She was dressed in her Sunday best: a powder pink suit, with a matching wide brimmed hat and a pink net that came down

24

over her face.

She burst out the chorus:

Then sings my soul,
My Saviour God, to Thee,
How great Thou art!
How great Thou art!

Kerry-Ann's eyes watered as she stifled a cough. Nana's perfume was *strong*. She held her breath and counted to see how long she could do it. Things started getting tricky around 35, and by 45 she blurted out her breath and gasped for air. Mum flashed her a look.

As soon as the service was over, they would go back to Nana's house. Grandpa would be there, watching the cricket as usual – but always with time for a chat with Kerry-Ann.

Nana's arms were wide, palms upwards, eyes fixed on the beams of the roof. Kerry-Ann followed her gaze.

At that moment she wouldn't have been surprised if Jesus himself had come down to punish her for thinking of cricket instead of praising

Him. She crossed herself. Just in case. Then the congregation knelt to pray.

But just as Kerry-Ann was about to start praying, the seed of an idea took root in her mind. Like a tiny plant it began to grow, its crisp green leaves unfurling and reaching upwards, growing stronger and stronger in the God-like light that bathed it.

She had it! She had a plan! A wide smile spread across her face.

Her eyes found her Nana, eyes shut, hands together, praying to the Lord.

Kerry-Ann crossed herself again and she mouthed her own word of 'thanks' to Jesus as she made her decision.

She knew exactly how she was going to deal with Moose.

CHAPTER FOUR

"Tank de Lord fi Jesus."

Nana sighed with relief as Mum finally turned the car into her street. The traffic had been slow and it was starting to rain. Mum pulled over at the kerbside.

"Kerry-Ann, dad will pick you up in an hour, OK? As soon as he gets off work. I've got the shopping to do."

"OK. Will you get me a —"

"Mango? If it's not too pricey. You be good now."

"'Course she'll be good, won't you mi darlin'?" said Nana.

The two of them climbed out of the car and Nana led Kerry-Ann up to the front door of her terraced brick house – the same house that Kerry-Ann's mum had grown up in.

As she entered, Kerry-Ann felt a wall of warm air and breathed in the familiar smell: mothballs,

Nana's perfume, but most importantly, Sunday dinner. Her stomach rumbled. Nana was miles better at cooking than Mum.

The soft deep-red carpet hugged her feet as she walked into the passageway and approached the kitchen. Its yellow walls were a stark difference to the damp, concrete-grey of outside.

Nana lifted the lid of a large pan that was sitting on the cooker. A cloud of steam rose and fogged up her glasses: coconut rice and kidney beans. She dipped in a spoon to taste it. Her eyes closed as she smacked her lips. Then she dipped in the spoon again, for another 'taste'.

"Where's Grandpa?"

Nana looked over to Kerry-Ann, her eyes appearing bigger through the high prescription glasses.

"Seebee? 'im asleep. He not feeling so good these days. But him soon come darlin'."

They went into the front room and Nana sat in her favourite armchair.

"Kerry-Ann. Go get yu Nana slippers fi me."

Kerry-Ann did as she was asked, finding the slippers in their usual place by the front door.

When she came back, Nana kicked off her shoes and wiggled her toes in front of the flames from the gas fire, before putting them into the slippers. Kerry-Ann wrinkled her nose.

"Go make yu Nana a cup-o-tea darlin."

Kerry-Ann suppressed a sigh. Nana was just in the kitchen. How hard would it have been to flip the kettle on?

She walked briskly to the kitchen and pulled out a large mug. Nana called to her.

"Kerry-Ann?"

"Yes Nana?"

"Hot water firs'. Den de milk."

"Yes Nana…"

"An' don't forget the sugar!"

"I won't Nana."

"Kerry-Ann?"

"Yes, Nana?" Kerry-Ann made an effort to keep her voice light and airy.

"Yu see the cupboard dere? The one with de

glass door?"

"Yes Nana…"

"A likkle bottle o'brandy in dere. Drop a likkle in the tea fi me."

How much was a little? Kerry-Ann decided it was about a teaspoon.

Once she made the tea with the brandy, she brought it in for Nana with a few Rich Tea biscuits.

"Thank yu mi darlin," Nana cupped the tea and balanced the saucer of biscuits on the armchair.

But as soon as she took a sip she screwed up her face.

"Where de brandy de?" She glared at Kerry-Ann. "Go get de bottle."

Moments later, Nana unscrewed the cap and poured a generous glug of the golden liquid into her tea, before taking a sip and sighing, satisfied.

Kerry-Ann sat. The sofa wheezed around her body, puffing her yellow skirt out.

As Nana sipped her tea, Kerry-Ann ran over it again in her mind. Her plan.

Moose was confident, entitled, arrogant – all

those things she found so annoying – but that meant he had a big weakness. A weakness that she would target.

Everything was on his side – he could book the club and she couldn't. If he booked up all the slots, she wouldn't be able to practise at all. He'd won.

But, she would challenge him to a match – his team against hers. Her friends against his. And it would be winner-takes-all: if he won, he could continue to book up the club. But, if she won, no more booking; just first to arrive gets the facilities – like now.

He should say no…but she reckoned he wouldn't be able to resist, not if she challenged him in front of everyone. His pride would be on the line. He'd never back down to a girl. And definitely not a girl like *her*. His arrogance would make him believe that he would win.

And to be fair, Moose's team was good. He was captain of the First XI so he'd have the club's best players on his side.

But Kerry-Ann was good too, wasn't she?

Younger than Moose, but she had the skills, she was sure of it! Well, almost sure. She just needed the chance to show it – and the time to get her best team together and practise every moment that they could. She would need to prepare carefully if this was going to work.

"What you thinking 'bout child?"

Nana interrupted her thoughts.

"Umm, just something I gotta do Nana. A cricket thing. But it's a bit…" she shrugged, not knowing how to explain her worries.

Nana smiled.

"Dem cricket tings yu all worry 'bout soo much! But what mi expect? Seebee been same way, ever since mi did know him. Dat even how we met!"

"Really?" asked Kerry-Ann. "What happened?"

"Well, maybe dis will cheer you up…" she began. "Mi did meet Seebee, when mi was jus' eight, and him was…erm…twelve? Someting like dat. Yu remember our friend So-So? Well – the one dat nowadays we call Limpin?"

"Yes…"

34

"He was dere. With Seebee and also, Killer and Mikey. An' no school. Mi c'yant remember why. So, group o' de pickney dem decide 'pon a game of cricket."

Flames from the gas fire whispered as they pumped out heat into the room, the rain got heavier and heavier, splattering on the glass, and the wind rattled Nana's loose window frames. This was going to be good. Kerry-Ann sank deeper into the sofa and as Nana began her story the scene appeared before her…

****

The simmering ball of fire hung low in the vast blue sky, its heat warming Seebee's skin. He was used to the heat, as were his friends. The boys gathered around their usual place – an open, grassy area – for the game. Seebee and So-So had got the word out. They would play a match here, before midday. Before the day reached its hottest.

Seebee's thickened, bare feet crunched onto

the parched grass. A crowd was gathering. Kids from the neighbourhood, and some from school. This was a match to watch. Even Mrs Rosie Bell's goat seemed interested as it stood near her fence, chewing grass and lazily casting its eyes over the pitch.

Seebee had challenged Pea Head and Bigman to a match. They were older, and more experienced, but Seebee always wanted to see where his skill could take him. Besides, he was fed up with Bigman and his friends pushing him around. As he and his crew strolled into the middle of the makeshift field, Bigman was already there, waiting.

"Mi tink yuh wudda stay home." Bigman shot some spit out of the gap in his teeth onto the grass. The boys with him smiled as they tried to intimidate Seebee.

Bigman was tall. Even for a 14. He had a tough life and it showed. His pinprick eyes squinted at Seebee and his toughened muscles popped out of his bare chest and arms. But Seebee stood his ground.

"Na man, mi ready for dis." Seebee answered.

Then he turned and gathered his team for a pre-match talk.

"Dis waah a serious ting," he insisted. "We need fi win. Bigman an dem deh boys dangerous. Eff dem win dem will run di school! Dat wah we want?"

His teammates shook their heads.

"Dat wah we want?!" Seebee reiterated, raising his hands animatedly at his line of players as if he was an army sergeant.

"Na man!" came the response from So-So, loud and clear. They were ready. Seebee had set his eyes on the prize. He needed to win. And when he had won, no longer would Bigman and his boys be rushing them in the playground.

Bigman's team was to bowl first. Seebee and So-So were the openers. Their opponents took their positions – wicket keeper, slip fielders, cover. Bigman would bowl. This was business.

Seebee glanced upwards at the cloudless blue sky. The wind kissed his cheeks, cooling his nervous sweats. His white vest was sticking to his skinny chest. Pulling it free and flapping it in the breeze, he muttered a quick prayer and discreetly crossed himself. And it was then that he saw them. Two black dots in the blue sky. Hovering. Circling. He knew that they were John Crows, and he knew that meant there was something dead nearby. It was a bad omen.

Determined not to let it rattle him, Seebee turned his mind to the game and prepared for Bigman's bowl. They were going to settle this like men. With cricket. The universal settler.

****

Nana took a noisy slurp of her tea, put her cup down and smiled at Kerry-Ann.

"Dem all spread out pon de grass. Ready fi play the game o de year. Bigman, him tek up his position for him run-up. Well back, yu know. Well, him do a long run. Him jump up, bowl the ball. And then…" Nana said dramatically, "on dat first bowl…dat ball *slap* up the goat inna de head!"

Nana slapped her hand on the sofa's arm so hard

that Kerry-Ann jumped.

"Him do one bleat. Just one cry. Then him clap," (She clapped her hands together) "and drop pon de ground. Dead!"

Nana stared at Kerry-Ann and chuckled at the memory.

"But what happened then?" gasped Kerry-Ann.

"Well," said Nana – and as she carried on the scene appeared before Kerry-Ann once again.

****

The boys fell silent. Seebee had sprinted off to do as many runs as he could, but soon slowed when he heard the howls and screams of the other boys around him. So-So took one look at the goat and bolted. Seebee called after him as he ran off across the grass, leapt over the barbed wire fence and disappeared down the dirt track. The rest of the team disintegrated right in front of his eyes. And when he took a closer look at the goat, he knew why.

This was Mrs Rosie Bell's very best goat. And everyone was scared of Mrs Rosie Bell – scared of her and her many sons.

Seebee felt sick. He looked up to the heavens seeking inspiration and saw two large, protruding eyes staring at him. A little girl, watching all the drama from a comfortable position up in a nearby tree.

"Wah yuh a do?" She called down, accusingly.

Her frog-like eyes blinked in the shade.

Seebee put his hands on his hips. The dead goat lay at his feet. To the left lay the cricket ball.

Bigman and his team had scattered. Of his friends, only Killer remained. Just him, Killer and this small girl in the tree.

****

Kerry-Ann interrupted her Nana.

"*You* were that girl in the tree?"

Nana nodded.

"Yes. And Seebee, him brave…" she said. "Mrs Rosie Bell was *fierce*. Him not fi worry about her

40

bwoy dem. Is *she* him fi worry 'bout!"

Nana chuckled again.

CHAPTER FIVE

Kerry-Ann heard footsteps in the passageway – slow and deliberate. Grandpa coming. His face lit up as soon as he saw her.

"Is how mi best girl?"

"I'm good, Grandpa."

Kerry-Ann jumped up to hug him, then made room for him on the sofa. Nana went out to make tea, and Kerry-Ann asked Grandpa how he was.

"So-So. Mi leg hurtin' jus here. Mi tired. But it good fi see yu. What you been up to?"

"Lots. Good stuff. But, Grandpa, I've got a problem. A cricket thing."

He nodded.

"Tell me."

So she did. Not everything, but the main point – that she had a really important game that she needed to win.

"Other team good?"

She nodded.

"Better dan you?"

"Maybe. I haven't played against them. But they're good."

He thought for a moment, then his face creased into a gentle smile.

"Dat is half de trick yu see? Y' haffi think you is good enough. Y'haffi believe it."

He tapped his finger on his forehead.

"Real cricket is played offa de pitch. It play in here. Yu see?"

She nodded.

"When you step up to the crease, it just you against de whole other team. Yu understan? You and your batting partner against the whole eleven…" he lowered his voice now. "But it also you against yourself Kerry-Ann. If you win de battle inna yu head, if you focus all your energy onto dat ball, you can hit a six every time," he smiled. "Or at least a four."

Kerry-Ann beamed back at him. She did get it – she knew exactly what Grandpa was talking about.

"Y'haffi practice as well. Me and mi friends used to practice all de time. You practice with yu team?"

"Every chance, Grandpa," she nodded.

"Good. Dat is good."

Nana returned and set down the tea.

"Thank you" smiled Grandpa. "Tell de story den na?"

So Nana carried on.

****

Seebee crouched low to look at the goat.

"Mrs Rosie Bell a guh dead yuh." The little girl in the tree gloated. "Ar one ah her sons. Shi haf nuff pickney dem."

Seebee considered running away. But the girl had seen him. He picked up the ball that had killed the goat. It was his cricket ball – his fault.

Killer strode up. He looked at the goat, at Seebee, and then back again at the goat.

"Wah wi a guh do?"

Seebee looked at him and shrugged his shoulders.

"Mi nuh know man." His voice trembled. He wished his big brother was here. Andsurd would know what to do.

Coughing to disguise his tears, he turned away so Killer and the girl wouldn't see.

"Yuh betta decide faas," a little voice piped up from the trees. Killer turned his face towards its branches.

"Hyacinth? Dat yu?" He peered upwards to the little girl.

"Wah happen, Killer."

"Wah yaah duh up dere?"

"Mi ago watch de game. Yu know how mi fi like de cricket so."

"Yeah man. Bad man game dat would've been ere so, y'know!" He exclaimed.

The little girl nodded her head in agreement.

Seebee looked incredulously from his friend to the girl as they chatted casually, as if Mrs Rosie Bell's dead goat wasn't lying right by their feet!

Didn't they know that if Mrs Rosie Bell found out what had happened, his life would not be worth living?

He considered leaving the goat where it was. There was already a fly buzzing round. Mrs Rosie Bell would just discover it dead when she came to bring it home. Then, she would soon find out about the game.

And Mrs Rosie Bell was fearsome. She would cuss him out in front of everyone. She had a stick that she kept on her veranda for the boys that dared to cheek her, and she was not afraid to use it.

He sighed heavily. He didn't want to face Mrs Rosie Bell, and he definitely didn't want to face her sons. He was stuck.

The small girl blinked down at him from her perch, understanding his predicament.

He wanted to leave, to run away like everyone else.

"What you gon do?" she asked again.

She looked down at him, waiting to see.

He shrugged, and turned, and began his long, lonely walk towards Mrs Rosie Bell's house to face his fate.

And above him, two black dots wheeled lower.
The John Crows had started to circle.

CHAPTER SIX

It was Monday lunchtime before Kerry-Ann and Amardeep finally got a few minutes to chat. They found a place on the bench in the playground, with kids screaming around them and playing football.

They watched as Michael Fincher scored, all eyes following the yellow ball as he booted it from the corner. It shot through the air, spinning as it went.

Kerry-Ann studied the boys, all running towards the ball. She could never understand how none of them seemed to pay attention to any rules.

As she bit into her ham sandwich, the ball flew into the back of the net, which folded and flapped as it accepted the golden gift. Boys roared in triumph, then ran back down the pitch congratulating each other as they went.

Amardeep had a cheese sandwich. Every day it was the same. When she asked him about it, he would just shrug one shoulder and say, "I like cheese."

What could she say to that? She completely understood. She liked ham.

And they both liked cricket.

On the pitch before them, studded boots raced towards exposed ankles and tackled anyone who got in their way. Of course, no one really managed to get possession.

Kerry-Ann took another bite and explained her plan to Amardeep.

He smiled.

"Knew you'd come up with something," he said, before adding: "Did you know, the longest cricket match ever, lasted 12 days?"

That one was easy. Kerry-Ann had read about that one way back.

Someone booted the ball to the other side of the pitch. The swarm of boys buzzed after it, scrabbling about, pushing and shoving.

"No girls," said Amardeep, nodding towards the football.

"Nah."

"Dunno why though."

They glanced at each other. And Kerry-Ann guessed what her friend was thinking.

Next year, when she reached thirteen, she wouldn't be able to play cricket at all. At least, not with Amardeep. The senior cricket team at their club wasn't mixed. Boys-only.

The games they were playing together now might be their last.

Amardeep seemed to be about to say something, but he sighed and shook his head.

Before he could speak, Kerry-Ann cut in.

"England–South Africa Test match in 1939. Lasted 12 days without a clear winner."

Then she added, "We've got a good plan – no way is Moose gonna kick us off the field."

And with that, she jumped up. It was time to issue the challenge.

****

After school, Kerry-Ann went straight home and thundered up the stairs. Her rucksack thudded down and she threw herself onto her bed.

Moose had taken the bait. Of course he had. Accepted the challenge without so much as a flinch. In fact, he seemed to relish it.

And why shouldn't he? Kerry-Ann had been full of confidence when she spoke to Amardeep. But could she really do this? What if they lost? What if she lost the chance to have a final season playing cricket with Amardeep and all her friends?

"Well," she said to herself, "we will just have to make sure that we don't lose!"

She deserved to win, didn't she? Moose was impossible. He had been impossible for years. Ever since…but she pushed the image away.

What happened to forgiveness? Mum was always going on about how important it is to forgive each other. Kerry-Ann wondered if it worked the same when you needed to forgive yourself.

And then another thought dropped. Not only had Moose not forgiven her. He never would.

All you have to do is apologise. The words slipped in through the back door of her mind. Stubbornly she shoved them out again. It was all too late. And she'd been young. It didn't count.

It counts to Moose…

No, not now! She and Amardeep had a match to win. This was important.

Besides, what good would an apology do?

Kerry-Ann focused her thoughts and began to draw up a list of friends she could rely on in her team. Time was short. Once she had names, she could bounce them off Amardeep.

****

Later that evening her phone buzzed. Amardeep – of course. She didn't tell him about how worried she felt about the whole situation. There was no point in both of them being nervous wrecks.

"Moose started this fight, but we'll finish it right? We can win, we've just got to believe in ourselves – that's what my grandpa reckons."

"You told him about it?"

"Sure. Well, sort of. I mean I told him it's a really big match, really crucial. And the other side is sure they'll win."

"Right…"

"But we can beat them Amardeep! If we are really confident. We're good. Grandpa said you don't win cricket on the pitch, you win in your own head."

"Yeah! I mean, probably…"

****

Amardeep wasn't sure, but he recognised her mood. She was excited and fired-up, and he didn't want to say the wrong thing here.

He didn't want to upset her. He hated it when they disagreed. It reminded him of when his Nan teased him.

"Beta, that one behaves just like your future wife!"

Amardeep had scowled at that comment, and dismissed it with a snort, but he knew that his Nan was no fool. And he also knew not to get on the wrong side of Kerry-Ann. Not when she was in this sort of mood.

She was still talking, still enthusiastic, trying to bring him with her. That was something he always loved about her – when you needed it most, Kerry-Ann had the positivity.

So – all they had to do was get a cracking team together, win the match, teach Moose, and his mates a lesson, and everything would work out. And at least they could play this last season together, before Kerry-Ann had to change clubs.

"OK, let's do it," he replied. "We'd better get our team together though – time's short, right?"

"Yeah, time's short," she laughed.

CHAPTER SEVEN

Kerry-Ann loved her grandparents, but she was still annoyed when Mum said she'd have to go back to their house the very next day after school – crucial time she could have spent practising for the match.

"Sorry love, but I'm working late and your dad will have gone off to work already. You can eat at Nana's – and you know how much they always like seeing you."

And they did.

"Hallo mi darling. Come give Nana a kiss."

Nana pushed her large, black rimmed glasses up her flat nose and enveloped Kerry-Ann in a hug. Normally, she would wriggle out of the crush, but today was different, maybe because of her worries about the coming match. Nana scooped her into her arms, and Kerry-Ann relaxed at the familiar warmth and the smell of mothballs.

"Yu want some sorrel? Mi 'ave some ready-made.

Seebee ah play dominoes when the boys arrive."

Kerry-Ann nodded eagerly. She loved sorrel. And watching Grandpa playing dominoes. He hadn't done that for a while. Or been to church. His brother, Andsurd had died the previous year and Mum said that it had made Grandpa "feel his age."

Nana gave her a side smile.

"Mi invite dem. Maybe Seebee will cheer up, if him have de boys round. Play a likkle record, shek a foot. Bring 'im outta all dis worry 'bout the past …him need fi stop worry so much…it na bring Andsurd back."

It was sweet the way that Nana looked out for Grandpa and Kerry-Ann always thought it funny that Nana referred to his friends as 'the boys' when they were old men!

Limpin was coming over with Killer. Kerry-Ann liked seeing them play – they always got excited – slamming down the dominoes, jumping out of their seats as if they were on fire and hopping around the room in excitement.

She kicked off her shoes in the hallway

and Nana went out to the garden, to look at her flowerbeds.

The sound of the television was blaring out loudly from the front room. Kerry-Ann put her head round the door.

"Hi Grandpa."

Grandpa looked up from the news, and smiled.

"Yu mudda drop yu off again?"

"Yeah…she's got a meeting or something."

"Meeting eh? That one always workin…" he whistled, shaking his head.

Kerry-Ann nodded.

"Back in a minute. Just going to the toilet."

She scampered up the stairs, not bothering with the light, and turned into the bathroom at the top.

But a few minutes later, when she came out, something caught her eye.

The bedroom door at the end of the landing was ajar, and soft lamp light was spilling onto the carpet.

"Grandpa?"

She smiled to herself and walked towards the bedroom door. The brass handle seemed to grow larger as if begging her to clasp it. She went in.

The red velvet curtains were drawn, and the single lamp just inside the door cast a faint, warm light over the patterned wallpaper. Grandpa wasn't there though.

This used to be Kerry-Ann's mum's room, but now it was just where things got stored. She'd found all kinds of stuff in here before – old photos, a jar full of old Jamaican money, wooden carvings of fish, rastamen and giraffes.

There was a tower of boxes stacked against the wall, pushed up against her Mum's old dressing table. She crossed over to the mirror, watching her reflection approach, and peered at the old photos taped around the edges. Photos of her mum, and her older sister, Kerry-Ann's Aunt Jackie. The two girls looked just like one another, same smiles, same expression, even similar clothes – the only difference seemed to be that Mum was shorter than her older sister.

There was one of Grandpa wearing a stetson hat, a young man then. He had a cigar in his mouth and was grinning. The photographer had caught him mid-laugh.

They must have been still fairly new in the country then, Kerry-Ann guessed. Something about Grandpa's fashion sense shouted "Jamaican country boy."

And then, she felt it. In the dimly lit room, she suddenly imagined that someone was singing to her – but it was more of a feeling than a sound, the feeling you get from listening to an old, favourite tune that you haven't heard in a while.

And there was a gentle chiming too, a muffled bell, as if from a clock buried under heaps of clothes. She stood still and listened, trying to guess which direction it was coming from.

Her mum's old bed had boxes piled on top, an old duvet folded neatly and a large fan laying sideways on it. But the noise was coming from underneath. Tentatively, Kerry-Ann crept towards the bed and crouched low. She peered underneath. It was dark. Dust motes stirred in front of her, like deep ocean fish suddenly disturbed. She stared, her eyes trying to focus.

And as she did, she saw them.

Two black, beady eyes staring back.

She startled and fell backwards. But it was just the toy badger! Her mum's old cuddly toy.

"Kerry-Ann?"

She heard Nana calling her from downstairs. And she noticed that her heart was racing, although she didn't know why – it was just a soft toy!

She laughed nervously, and now Nana's footsteps were on the stairs.

Thump, thump, thump…

"Did you fall, darlin'? You alright?"

Thump, thump, thump…

Suddenly, Kerry-Ann had an urge to hide, like she used to when she was little. And she didn't want Nana to find her in here.

She looked around – maybe behind the boxes? No, there wasn't enough room. Behind the curtains? That was always a fantastic hiding place, but no, she was bigger now and her feet would poke out at the bottom.

Thump, thump, thump…

The wardrobe! Kerry-Ann ducked over and squeezed inside.

Thump, thump, thu—

The doorknob squeaked and Nana stepped into the room.

"Kerry-Ann?" Nana stopped. She looked around the room confused.

Then she chuckled.

"Yuh think yu mudda never hide from mi? Dis not new – I got yu…"

Nana came straight over to the wardrobe, pulled the handle and…

Kerry-Ann stared out from her hiding place. Nana was not moving, not even blinking. She was as still as a statue and her glasses had become dark holes, through which Kerry-Ann could feel her frozen gaze. The air itself seemed frozen too, even the motes of dust. The strange chimes were louder than ever.

Kerry-Ann swung the wardrobe door fully open. Nothing else moved.

She climbed out, squeezing past her statue-like Nana.

Then she noticed a soft glow: something was pulsing, underneath the bed.

And she knew, even before she leaned down to look, what she would see.

The toy badger was still there. It was looking straight up at her, holding her in its gaze.

Then something came rolling out from under the bed. There was no mistaking the red blur, the smooth round body, its yellowing seam used as a rudder, directing it to where the bowler wanted it to go.

It was spinning, rolling towards her.

And just before the cricket ball touched her hand, Kerry-Ann thought of the cork inside it, of the layers of twine wound-around the leather casing.

And the next moment the bed, the room, and everything around her vanished.

CHAPTER EIGHT

The air was warm. Birds were singing and a gentle breeze was stirring. Kerry-Ann breathed, slow and deep, as she stirred from the dark depths of her dream.

It was a Sunday. Of this, she was sure.

Church day. But Mum hadn't come in yet to wake her, so she lay there enjoying the peace while it lasted.

Gradually, the warmth on her inner eyelids turned from yellow to orange.

And in a part of her mind, she realised that she was not in bed.

She felt a warm breeze on her cheeks and opened her eyes a crack. The wind was rippling through the tops of the trees. Kerry-Ann saw them turning up their pale undersides in greeting as the breeze touched the high boughs. Voices rose and fell. And then there was the unmistakable sound of a cricket ball hitting a bat.

Her hand instinctively reached out for her glasses on her bedside table – but all she grasped was air. And she realised where her glasses were – on her nose. She opened her eyes fully, and looked around.

She was lying on a bench, in a park.

A cricket game was playing out in front of her. The sun was hot, and high in the sky...but the sky was grey.

Everything, all around her, was a shade of grey.

She was dreaming. Wasn't she?

A cricket ball came bouncing towards her and a boy came running after it. He grabbed the ball and threw it back with a strong left arm. The ball shot forwards, spinning as it went. Then he turned to Kerry-Ann. Their eyes met, and the world changed.

Like dipping a loaded paintbrush in a pot of clear water, clouds of colour flooded and rolled in all directions. Indigos and greens drenched everything. Kerry-Ann gasped at the sudden injection of colour, in all its glory, as it dripped off everything, above, below, around her.

The boy's face came into sharp focus. His tight

afro was cut close to his head and his hairline was neatly trimmed.

"Yu alright?" he said, turning towards her, but also keeping an eye on the game.

Kerry-Ann stared at him; it was as if a black and white picture was coming to life, climbing out of a frame, and walking around in front of her in full colour.

She sat up, smiled and nodded – stunned to silence as his face turned from grey to brown.

Walking backwards, still watching Kerry-Ann with a concerned look on his face, the boy held her gaze for a moment longer before turning around and trotting to join his teammates.

There was yelling and whooping as he ran back. Boys and young men surrounded him and gave him celebratory slaps on his back. The air echoed with the smacking of high fives all round.

In Kerry-Ann's mind's eye, she saw the badger's spinning black glassy eyes. And she knew.

She was still in London. She knew this boy. But she knew him in another time.

The young man with the cricket bat, laughing with his friends. This was Seebee – her Grandpa.

She had travelled to the past.

Her heart was racing, but not with fear – not quite – she didn't know why, but she felt more excited than afraid.

She stretched and breathed deep.

The cricketers had stopped playing – the game was over.

The tall boy with his bat and ball was chatting with his friends and they were walking away, towards the road, away from the park.

And Kerry-Ann understood. She was meant to be here, and she was meant to follow them.

CHAPTER NINE

On the road, the group of boys halted.

"So-So, mi see you later."

Two of the group were saying goodbye. Their pink palms slid together in a skin-to-skin handshake as the slightly taller boy turned down a side road.

"Later Seebee."

The boys continued walking, chatting about their cricket game, and how they were going to a party later on. There were high fives and skin slaps all round before the group folded away to just one. Grandpa.

He gave her a side eye and pretended not to notice her following him.

Ten minutes later, Seebee squeaked open an iron gate and walked up to his front door. Kerry-Ann halted.

"Er…can mi help yu wi someting?" he said, suddenly spinning around, properly acknowledging her for the first time since the bench.

"Er…yes…please."

Seebee waited for her to elaborate, but before she could speak again, the front door opened.

In the darkened doorway was a woman wearing a blue floral dress.

"Seebee…" she said, more in confirmation than greeting. Her voice was deep and there was a tiredness in her eyes. She coughed as she saw Kerry-Ann hovering nearby. "Who a yuh friend?" she asked, stepping to the side as Seebee squeezed past her body. He muttered something that Kerry-Ann didn't quite hear.

The woman stared at Kerry-Ann. This was clearly Seebee's mother. They had the same nose, the same wide, open face and soft brown eyes.

Kerry-Ann also recognised the same challenging expression that she sometimes saw on her Grandpa's face.

But as the two of them looked at each other Kerry-Ann felt that tingle again – and she saw the badger in her mind's eye, with its swirling black eyes. She shivered.

And at the same moment Seebee's mother's face changed from quizzical, to soft. She seemed to visibly relax.

"Come na? Yu hungry? Pickney dem always hungry…"

She smiled as she stepped aside and allowed Kerry-Ann in.

Entering, Kerry-Ann headed down the short passageway and saw Seebee again, now in the kitchen. Light streamed in. There was an older boy sitting with him – his brother, Andsurd? – and a young woman with braids. Her chair was pulled up opposite them at the small square table.

"Andsurd yu leavin'?" Seebee was saying.

"Yeah man, places to go, people to see."

He smiled, a wide, bright, cheerful grin.

"Can mi borrow yu bat?"

"Yu playin' again?"

"Yeah man, aimin' to."

Andsurd patted the younger boy's shoulder.

"Always playin' Seebee. Bat in mi room. Look

after it brudda. Yu know mi bring it from home."

"Thanks man."

And then he was gone – with a nod to the young woman and Kerry-Ann – still smiling as he ducked through the door. Wherever he was going, it was somewhere he really wanted to be.

Seebee followed his brother out, and Kerry-Ann heard him taking the stairs, two at a time.

Kerry-Ann was left alone with the older woman who she guessed must be her great grandma, and the young woman with braids. That must be her great aunt.

She was shuffling her papers, making a more presentable pile. Curious, Kerry-Ann approached. The young woman had perched her pencil behind her ear, and was concentrating on a maths problem on one of the papers.

She looked up at Kerry-Ann.

"Are you gonna just stand there staring at me?"

"Huh?"

The young woman rolled her eyes and pushed the chair out with her foot for Kerry-Ann to sit on.

"Where have you come from anyway?" she asked.

Seebee's mum had started humming a song while she stirred something in the pot. Stew, Kerry-Ann guessed. The kitchen soon became full of a glorious spicy smell, and her tummy rumbled.

"Erm…?"

For a moment, Kerry-Ann couldn't think of what to say. Somehow saying that she came from the 21st century, transported through time by a toy badger with beady, black spinning eyes and grasping claws, didn't quite seem right!

The young woman however, was expecting an answer.

"Just the park. I bumped into Seebee and…" Kerry-Ann trailed off as, suddenly, the young woman's face relaxed, just like her great grandma's had moments before. Kerry-Ann felt the tingle of the badger's magic once again. The young woman smiled.

"Well," she said. "I'm Sandra."

"Hang on!" she said, "You're not Seebee's *girlfriend* are you?"

Kerry-Ann shook her head vehemently. The young woman chuckled.

"Just checking."

Smiling, she pulled out a heavy text book from a bag underneath the table and flicked her braids. The beads, three to a braid, were in the colours of the Jamaican flag: black, green and gold.

She saw Kerry-Ann watching, and grinned.

"If you hang around I can do yours if you like?"
Kerry-Ann nodded.

In Kerry-Ann's time, this young woman had died as an old lady. Now Kerry-Ann was literally in front of her, she could see that her great aunt Sandra was about ten years older than Seebee. She must be around 25.

Kerry-Ann tried to think of something else to say, but found that she didn't need to – great grandma bustled over with a steaming bowl of stew chicken.

"You hungry, child?"

She nodded. She was really hungry.

"Mi did think so. Dey not feeding yu right…"

And Sandra smiled as Kerry-Ann began eating –
as hungrily as if she hadn't had a meal in years.

"Mmmm this is good…really good…"

"Know what that is, Kerry-Ann?" said Sandra.

"Stew chicken?"

"Nope. It's the taste of home."

"Right!"

And they laughed together – and whether it
was some magic from the badger, or the effect of
the food, or just what happens if you travel back
time and meet your own family – Kerry-Ann felt
accepted, without questions. She belonged in this
room, in this house, with these people.

****

Later on, Kerry-Ann lay on a squeaky
fold-up bed. She'd been invited to stay and was in
the corner of Sandra's room. The darkness was
heavy. There was no sound of traffic outside, but in
the distance she could hear what she guessed must
be trains – steam trains, chuffing along London's rail
lines.

And the room felt homely, but also unfamiliar, and far away from home.

She wondered what her Mum was doing. Was everyone worried about her? Were they looking? Had they called the police?

No, she told herself, that didn't make sense.

When she returned to her own time – and she was sure that she would – it would probably be at exactly the same moment as she had left. That's how time travel worked, didn't it? In the stories? You could be away for weeks, but in your own world it was only seconds.

That's probably how this would work too, when the badger decided to return her home. Or when she told the badger she wanted to go.

But when would that be?

She thought about Amardeep again, and the coming battle with Moose. And she smiled as she thought about how much she'd enjoyed watching Grandpa – young Grandpa – playing with his friends.

This is where she'd learn how to win her game.

Here, she could see Grandpa's advice in action. And once she had discovered the secret, she'd go back home.

CHAPTER TEN

In the morning, Kerry-Ann was woken by her great grandma's singing. It was a song that Kerry-Ann recognised. She had heard her own Nana singing it several times.

When the Saints go marching in
When the Saints go marching in
Oh Lord, how I want to be in that number!
When the Saints go marching in!

The smell of frying bacon wafted up the stairs. Her stomach growled.

Next to her bed were her clothes from the day before. She pulled on her jeans and her t-shirt (now a bit dirtier and a bit sweatier too) and made her way downstairs towards the singing.

Sandra was at the kitchen table, reading a piece of folded paper.

"Morning sleepy head," she said in between mouthfuls of porridge.

Kerry-Ann's great grandma, who was frying the

bacon along with some plantain, dished her up a plate.

"Where's Seebee?" Kerry-Ann asked. It felt weird to be calling him that.

Sandra rolled her eyes and leaned towards her.

"Here's the thing you need to understand about Seebee," she said, while waving her spoon around. "The only thing he thinks about is cricket. The only things he sees are things to do with cricket, and the only thing he hears are the sounds of someone – *anyone* – playing cricket. And then he just has to join in."

She took another spoon of porridge.

"Sometin' wrong wid dad bwoy!" she said, switching to a strong Jamaican accent. "There's no talking to him about anything else, anything important."

Sandra picked up a piece of paper from the table and waved it under Kerry-Ann's nose.

"Like this! The struggle. We all need to play our part."

Shaking her head, she took another mouthful.

Her beads tinkled as her head moved animatedly.

Kerry-Ann looked at the piece of paper. It spoke of black people marching on the other side of London, in Notting Hill. On the front was a drawing of a woman holding up a sign: "United We Stand, Divided We Fall."

"Cricket isn't going to get us equal rights. Cricket isn't going to make them sit up and take notice. Cricket..." Sandra huffed. "It's just a stupid game."

Kerry-Ann stabbed a piece of plantain with her fork and shoved it into her mouth. It tasted so good.

But Sandra interrupted her enjoyment.

"You should come," she said. "If we want change, we have to make it for ourselves," then she pointed to the pamphlet with her milk-soaked spoon. "That, right there..." she said with her mouth full.

Kerry-Ann looked again at the image. Behind the woman, in the background, were pictures of young white men with odd hairstyles and funny shoes.

"Them..." she said, "Teddy Boys. I heard this

story once where they strapped this black man to the back of their car and then drove at speed 'til his body just…" Sandra shook her head.

Kerry-Ann's eyes grew wide. Her great grandma came over to the table and sat down with a cup of tea.

"Sandra, don't frighten de pickney."

"She ought to know what we are facing Mum. We need to be united."

"Yes. Mi no you right, Sandra, but mek de pickney enjoy her breakfast firs na man?"

Sandra spooned more porridge in with her right hand and grabbed a piece of toast with her left. She was ready to go, off to meet others involved in the march. Kerry-Ann thought about what she wanted: to watch her Grandpa play cricket. All this stuff Sandra was saying was bad and everything, but it didn't really have anything to do with her.

"Where did you say Seebee was?" Kerry-Ann asked.

"At de park…him and him friend dem gone fi play," her great grandma replied.

Kerry-Ann sprung up out of her seat. She wanted to see her grandpa play again and she needed to learn everything she could from him, while she was here.

"Erm…I forgot, I am supposed to be there too…but, thanks for breakfast," she said. She jumped up and dashed through the passageway and out the front door.

Sandra shrugged, grabbed a rasher of bacon from Kerry-Ann's plate and took a bite. After all, she was concerned about having a hearty breakfast to set her up for the day's marching. Standing up for oneself usually left one extremely hungry.

CHAPTER ELEVEN

Kerry-Ann arrived at the park puffing and out of breath. She spotted Grandpa and his friends straight away – a group of black, athletic teenagers and young men – enjoying a serious game of cricket among the picnicking families and couples strolling in the morning sunshine.

Seebee was bowling. He took a short run up, just 5 or 6 paces. The ball left his hand smoothly and went flying in the direction of the batsman.

Kerry-Ann watched. Did Seebee rely on pace or was he a bowler that would spin? Her gut told her that her Grandpa would be one to spin the ball. It would require more technique, so knowing her Grandpa, he would pride himself on being able to spin.

She watched, her eyes glued to the ball. It was hurtling through the air but somehow, she seemed to see it in slow motion. When she squinted, it was as if her eyes did a zoom thing, and she could see it up close. And it was spinning. It was spinning so fast it was almost a blur. Kerry-Ann grinned. The ball swung in and hit the stump square on – the batsman had missed it. Someone yelled "Out!" and Grandpa leapt up in celebration.

"Yeah man Seebee!" a fielder called, running up to him and slapping him on the back. Seebee laughed. Kerry-Ann moved closer. He saw her and sauntered over.

"Whaapen?"

"Oh er…hi… "

"Yu nuh 'ave a home fi go to?"

"Nope." Kerry-Ann grinned mischievously. Seebee raised his eyebrows.

"Is who' yu frien' Seebee?," one of the players called out.

"She nah me frien," he said, but seeing the expectant expressions of the other boys, he reluctantly introduced them.

"Dis mi boys dem. Dem call dis one Live Drive,

and dis one Trojan."

"Oh right…er cool names!"

Seebee rolled his eyes.

"What dey call yu?" Live Drive said suspiciously, one eyebrow raised. He was taller than the others, and looked more like an adult.

"I'm Kerry-Ann."

The boys stood in silence as if weighing her up. Kerry-Ann tried to think of something to say. She wasn't sure why, but Grandpa's domino match popped into her head.

"Which one is Limpin? And Killer?"

"Mi na know no Limpin," said Sebee, "but dat over there is Killer."

Kerry-Ann followed his gaze. So, that was Killer. The one from Nana's story. And, in later life, still one of Grandpa's good friends.

Behind him she saw a face that she thought she recognised, even though it was younger and had a lot more hair – it looked like a young Limpin…But maybe she was wrong – Seebee had said he didn't know a Limpin…

Killer was signalling to the boys to re-join the game and they trotted back towards him.

Kerry-Ann watched from the boundary as batsman after batsman stepped up and bowler after bowler aimed for wickets. Off-cutters, bouncers, in-swingers – a wide range of techniques were tried.

All the players were dressed in cricket whites. They looked professional on the bright green velvet grass. The silver birches swished in the wind, their leaves dancing, flashing their lighter undersides at Kerry-Ann as she stared into the dark branches that grew strong and bold up into the stretching blue sky.

Soon, the teams swapped, and Seebee was on the batting side. He picked up his bat – the one that Andsurd had lent him – and walked into the middle and took his place confidently at the crease. The bat shimmered in the heat.

Seebee was still and focussed as he tried to predict what the bowler was going to do. The first ball hurtled towards him. Seebee's eyes remained fixed on the ball as he judged its line and length. With perfect timing he rotated his body and brought up his bat to meet it.

THWACK!

The bat smacked the ball head on and it was thrown far across the field and beyond the boundary. A six.

A fielder retrieved the ball and threw it back in to the bowler. The bowler ran up again and once again the ball flew towards Grandpa.

And this time, Kerry-Ann was ready. If Seebee could predict the bowler, Kerry-Ann could predict her Grandpa. She knew he'd play offensively – and another pull shot made sense of the bowler's delivery. But with the opposing team's fielders now forewarned, he would place the ball in a different spot, further down the field. Before the ball left the bowler's hand she was on the move. Her legs pounded, arms pumped, as she sprinted. She positioned herself in just the right spot so that the ball seemed to come whizzing towards her, landing neatly in her cupped hands.

Killer, Live Drive, Trojan and So-So stared in disbelief. Kerry-Ann's heart pounded in her chest.

"She c'yan't do that. We no play with girls," she heard the boys whispering, and then one yelled, "Hey! You c'yan't do dat!"

Kerry-Ann grinned while tossing the ball and catching it again in her left hand.

"Just did mate!" she replied, enjoying the shocked look on their faces. Seebee came over to her.

"Where you learn fi play like dat?"

Kerry-Ann beamed.

"My grandpa taught me. How about I join in?"

So-So started shouting from the sides.

"Yuh c'yan't let her play! She a girl!"

Kerry-Ann stared at him.

"And? Your point is?"

Kerry-Ann grinned again and turned to Seebee. "Bet I can bowl you out in three." Seebee narrowed his eyes, while the boys drew closer.

"What's the matter? Afraid I will show you up in front of your friends?"

"What? Nah man! It's mi dat will show yu up!"

But he sounded less certain. Kerry-Ann strolled towards the pitch.

"Yuh a guh play her Seebee?" Killer questioned, as Seebee walked past him and stood at the crease. "Seebee?"

"Gwaan na man!" he yelled at him.

Killer watched, incredulous, as this slight girl stood in front of the wickets, tossing the cricket ball. Seebee looked determined, his mouth stretched into a thin line. Killer took his position opposite his batting partner.

Seebee and Kerry-Ann eyed each other and Kerry-Ann wondered what kind of bowl she should make. Grandpa had taught her to fast bowl, but to use it against him now would be? Unfair? Or serendipity? He wouldn't be expecting it. Not on her first bowl. Not from a girl. It was almost too good. She had to use it.

Seebee tapped his bat on the ground, and looked towards Kerry-Ann, nodding his head slightly to let her know he was ready. Kerry-Ann made up her mind what to do.

As she stepped backwards to create her running space, she envisaged what her body needed to do: she needed a comfortable run-up and proper hip-shoulder separation, as well as a stable wrist. She rolled her wrists in a mini warm up. Focus. It was all about balance and precision. She took a deep breath and launched herself.

Her legs and arms pounded in rhythm, her balance felt good. She looked directly at the stumps.

The ball shot towards Seebee. Too late, he realised what he was facing. Stepping his knee forward he lifted his bat, but he was too slow. The ball flew past him and smashed the stumps. The bails fell. Everyone watched on in silence as they clattered to the floor. Then, suddenly, Trojan began to laugh. Bowled out for a duck. Killer strode towards her smiling.

"Is weh yuh learn fi do dat?"

"I told ya. My grandpa."

Kerry-Ann grinned. Seebee approached her and held out his hand to shake. She clasped it.

"Yu grandpa good," he said smiling. Kerry-Ann grinned back.

The day seemed to fly by. The best day's cricket of Kerry-Ann's life. She drank in every detail, storing up all of Grandpa's moves.

All too soon the sun began to set and although it wasn't dark, the temperature had cooled and the teams decided that it was time to call it a day. Seebee and his friends stood on the field talking while others drifted. He put his bat away in a kit bag.

"Come fi mi yard" Trojan said, as he flung his bag over his back.

"De music gonna be sweet and it nuh tek long fi tek de bus. Straight to Notting Hill."

He stuffed his sweater into his bag – Kerry Ann could see that it was heavy and contained more than just his cricket whites.

"A'right," said Seebee. "But mi beg you. If yu see me a talk to Hyasinth na badder me like last time. Me tell yu. Dat my girl dat! She just don't know it yet!" He laughed loud.

"Yu a come So-So?" Killer asked. So-So shrugged his shoulders.

"Mi will come along but me na know if me a stay."

Killer shook his head.

"Yu know So-So, yu name is too right. Yu never good. Yu never bad. Always So-So!"

They all laughed as they began to walk to the road that ran alongside the park.

"Yu'ah come?" Killer asked Kerry-Ann. Trojan, So-So and Seebee turned to see her answer.

"Obvs…" she grinned as she fell in line with their steps.

The five boys: Seebee, Killer, Trojan, Live Drive and So-So walked to the bus stop with Kerry-Ann in the middle. Suddenly Killer turned to Kerry-Ann.

"Yu dance?"

"Er…dance?"

"Yeah man! Dance!" He said, grinning excitedly. The other four boys stopped and turned to face Kerry-Ann.

"Seebee The Cool Fool…." He gestured towards Seebee who took a reluctant bow. "The Live Drive and the Trojan."

Live Drive spun around as if he was on a dance floor and Trojan just grunted. "We ah go look cris tonight!"

Killer opened his bag and took out what he was dying to show off: polished, black dancing shoes. To Kerry-Ann the toe seemed to be sharpened to a point.

He caressed his shoes as he gestured for Kerry-Ann to come closer. But as she reached out a hand to touch them he abruptly pulled it back and said in all seriousness, "na touch man, na touch."

Just at that moment, the bus arrived and all five, with Kerry-Ann trailing on as a half-accepted sixth member, hopped on at the back. They boys were in good spirits as they climbed the narrow winding stairs to the top.

"Mi ah love London…" So-So said while looking down at the people walking on the streets.

"Yeah man!" Killer agreed. "It na bad. Na bad at all. An plenty green fi play cricket. Hey, Seebee, yu remember dat time back home, when dat ball lick up Mrs Rosie Bell goat?" Killer burst out laughing. Seebee chuckled sheepishly, but for him the memory was still too fresh. His dad had attempted to salvage the situation by using his machete to chop up the goat into pieces for Mrs Rosie Bell. Sort of a peace offering. And it had sort of worked.

Even so, Seebee had still had to work off what they thought the goat was worth, running errands. It had taken him over three months to square things.

"Mrs Rosie Bell – she was scary man…" Seebee shook his head.

"Yu did pay de debt though," said So-So. "Yu did the right ting man."

You did the right thing… Kerry-Ann thought suddenly about Moose, about his mother, and what had happened. But that wasn't the same, was it? She'd been much younger…

The boys were laughing again.

"London, is definitely fi me. Me nah go home yet. Me ago mek me fortune firs," So-So said again.

Just then, The Live Drive started singing - about London, and how it was their city. Where they wanted to be.

The boys grinned and they all joined in at the top of their voices.

Kerry-Ann watched, smiling as she saw her grandpa and his friends, singing the Lord Kitchener song that she had only seen on a black and white documentary that her mum made her watch. This was history! She forgot all about her battle with Moose – their unfinished business – and joined in with the song.

******

It was dusk when they arrived in Notting Hill. And it was only when they had hopped off and Kerry-Ann saw the crowds that she remembered Sandra and her pamphlet.

There were knots of people everywhere, some holding banners, some chatting, but all looking serious and determined.

When some of the protestors moved off to begin the march, the crowd thinned – and Kerry-Ann saw some white men who looked exactly like the ones on the pamphlet that Sandra had shown her. Her stomach flipped in fear. Teddy Boys.

CHAPTER TWELVE

Kerry-Ann stood between So-So, Killer, Seebee and Live Drive. The blood drained from her face as she stared at the Teddy Boys opposite her.

The march went on. People buzzed and flowed around them, intent on joining the protest, but the Teddy Boys were closing in on the friends. Kerry-Ann felt sweat trickle down her face. She was poised, ready to fight or run. She wasn't quite sure which.

In the swell of bodies, nobody else seemed to notice what was happening. A Teddy Boy with a floppy fringe rolled in the shape of a V, looked directly at Seebee and pulled out a bicycle chain. Kerry-Ann could see Seebee trembling as he forced his mouth into a thin, stubborn line. She could feel his bravery. Instinctively, she positioned her body slightly in front of her young grandpa.

Playfully swinging the chain, a cold smile spread

over the Teddy Boy's face and he took a boxer's position, stretching his skinny trousers to capacity. His pristine white jacket hung on him perfectly. All the Teddy Boys were dressed smartly in suits, outfits that jarred with their weapons and intentions. Seebee reached out his hand, rested it protectively on Kerry-Ann's shoulder and whispered so only she could hear.

"Yu nah fi worry yu hear? Dis 'here ting nothin'. Scuffle break out alla de time. But if mi tell yu fi run? Yu run."

"Well, well, well!"

One of the Teddy Boys called out, and stepped forward, cracking his knuckles. "Looks like we have a little outing? A bit late for a little girl to be out, ain't it?"

His attention was now completely on Kerry-Ann. She felt exposed under his sharp gaze. She lifted her fists. The Teddy Boy laughed.

"We don't want no trouble," Live Drive yelled through the noise of the crowd. But the Teddy Boys laughed again. One of them had a cruel, sword-like knife protruding from the belt of his trousers.

"Well, you should've stayed in your own country then."

"Dis is our country!" So-So yelled.

"You're 'avin' a laugh ain't ya? England is a white country. And I hate to tell you mate, but you ain't white. You don't belong here. You ain't welcome here. And we…" he gestured to his friends as they slowly began to walk closer, "are gonna make sure the message is driven all the way back home. Right back to Africa." The crowd around them was becoming thick with bodies again, as more and more protestors – men and women of all ages – joined the demonstration from the surrounding side streets. Sensing the advantage, Seebee yelled to Kerry-Ann and his friends, "let's move!"

Live Drive and So-So headed off in one direction and Killer, Seebee and Kerry-Ann went in another. The Teddy Boys split up too, the one with the knife going after So-So and Live Drive. The friends were safe for now, sheltering among the marchers with their banners held high and people shouting slogans. But scuffles had begun to break out, and the four Teddy Boys were slipping in and around the protestors, searching for their teenage targets, pushing and shoving and shouting things about black people that Kerry-Ann couldn't hear but knew were bad.

They were all running now, desperate to get away.

Kerry-Ann's heart was thumping so hard she thought it would burst out of her chest. She stopped, catching her breath. Seebee saw that she wasn't moving. He called after her.

"Mi say run!"

But then she saw the white suit – the Teddy Boy with the bicycle chain. He was in the middle of a scuffle, but at that moment he looked up and locked eyes on Kerry-Ann.

To Kerry-Ann it seemed as if the crowd parted, allowing him to stride towards her, chain swinging low. She ran, ran, ran down the street, Seebee at her side.

The Teddy Boy yelled at them. "Oi!"

But Kerry-Ann didn't turn around.

Seebee rounded a corner and Kerry-Ann followed. The crowd was busier here and Seebee ploughed straight into a line of people with placards. He was pushed roughly to the side by compacted bodies and fell to the ground, calling out in pain.

Kerry-Ann desperately tried to pick him up before the Teddy Boy caught up with them.

"Can you get up?" she shouted. An older man stopping to help, reached out and lifted Seebee up, knocking his kit bag off his shoulder. And as it clattered onto the street, his bat fell out. Kerry-Ann instinctively grabbed both the bag and the bat. Then the Teddy Boy rounded the corner and saw them.

CHAPTER THIRTEEN

The Teddy Boy launched himself at Kerry-Ann and Seebee, yelling. Kerry-Ann was terrified. But even in that moment, that moment when her teenage grandpa was hurt, when an angry white racist was hurling himself at her, wielding a weapon at a march in 1958, Kerry-Ann realised.

They had already won this fight! She knew they had. It had already happened. And now, right there in the chaos of the fighting and the screaming and the pain and the hatred, she knew. This was her London. This was her home. The Teddy Boys had lost and the marchers had won.

But right now, the Teddy Boy was swinging the bicycle chain above his head and moving fast.

Seebee yelled in fear but it was Kerry-Ann who the Teddy Boy reached first. And just as she was thinking that the right people had already won this battle, he struck.

The bicycle chain swung towards her head, the heavy metal singing through the air. Instinctively, Kerry-Ann raised the cricket bat to protect herself and the chain made contact.

Kerry-Ann fell to the floor. She stared at her attacker as he rolled up his fist. She wanted to scream, but nothing came out. Her vision swam and in her mind's eye she suddenly saw the badger's swirling black eyes holding her in a spinning pool of darkness.

The fist was pulling back. The young man's muscled arm was tensing for the blow.

But the blow didn't land.

Instead, there was a crackling and snapping noise. One minute Kerry-Ann was on the ground and the next — she was gone.

The Teddy Boy's fist grew slack.

Seebee's mouth hung open. He blinked in shock, staring at the empty space where the girl had been lying. There was nothing there. Nothing but a blackened stain on the concrete, curling smoke and the faint smell of burning leather.

CHAPTER FOURTEEN

Nana held the wardrobe door open. Then she laughed.

"Found you!"

Kerry-Ann blinked up at her – for a moment confused, until the warmth, and comforting smells of Nana's home enveloped her once again.

"Hide-n-seek, eh? Not too old?"

Nana wrapped her in a hug. And Kerry-Ann closed her eyes, and enjoyed the feeling of love. She was home, where she belonged. Safe.

From downstairs, the doorbell rang.

"Come na?" said Nana. "Let's see who dat."

Kerry-Ann went ahead to look.

It was Grandpa's friends. Limpin, Trojan and Killer.

Kerry-Ann grinned and threw herself into them. She was so relieved they were alive, and all in one piece! Her trip through time hadn't changed things.

Limpin was taken aback but soon embraced

her. Kerry-Ann had just seen them being chased by crazed racists – but Nana's hug and the sight of Granpa safe and sound was already beginning to make it feel like a distant memory.

"Come in na man!" Grandpa yelled from the front room as Nana, still smiling, was coming down the stairs to greet the guests.

As Kerry-Ann watched, Limpin – who had been the young So-So back in the past – used his crutch to get along the corridor. She thought about the Teddy Boys chasing after him and their weapon of choice: a knife.

"Whaapen brudda!?" Killer greeted grandpa with a hand slap and then they slid palms.

"Yah man…mi alright."

"Yu boys wan some sorrel?" Nana called from the kitchen. Trojan put his head round the door to look at Nana beside the open fridge door.

"Wha? Come on na man! Tek out de brandy yu av pon de cupboard dere. In fact, bring de rum. Dominoes is a serious ting!"

Kerry-Ann sipped her sorrel as the old men set

up their game.

Nana smiled as Trojan and Killer went to the kitchen to get a fold-up table they knew Nana had stored in a cupboard by the back door. They set up the game.

Soon enough, Kerry-Ann was watching the four old men roaring with laughter.

****

Later that evening, after a lot of dominoes, a lot of food, and a lot rum too, Grandpa's friends took a taxi home. Nana had retired to the front room to read her book.

Grandpa and Kerry-Ann were washing the dishes when Kerry-Ann told him.

"Grandpa?"

"Yes darlin?"

"I was in Mum's old room."

"Yes."

"And, well I think I found your old cricket bat. I mean, the one you had when you were younger? Andsurd's bat."

Kerry-Ann glanced at her grandpa and she saw his eyes widen – the same expression that she'd seen on the young Seebee's face, just hours earlier.

"Yu must be seein' 'tings Kerry-Ann," he laughed and shook his head. "Dat bat long gone."

"No Grandpa, honest, I think I found it upstairs – I'll show you –"

And before he could protest, she sprinted off up to the room, to fetch it. She couldn't keep the smile off her face as she ran back down to give it to him.

Grandpa stared – he stood there astonished as Kerry-Ann pressed the bat into his hands. He opened his mouth, but no words came out.

"It is isn't it? Andsurd's bat?"

"It is Kerry-Ann – the same –" his voice a hoarse whisper, "but how you find it? I lost this years ago."

"Do you remember how you lost it?"

Grandpa sank into a chair.

"Well, mi was just a likkle older than yu, when mi lose dat bat. Me erm…" he rubbed his hands together awkwardly. "Dere was a likkle ruckus. Up at Notting Hill. Dere was one likkle pickney dere."

He gave Kerry-Ann a side glance.

"Mi nah remember her name. She disappear as fast as she come. But…" again he glanced at Kerry-Ann, looking as if he sort of recognised her but couldn't quite place her face. "Me did think she took mi bat."

"What happened? That night?" Kerry-Ann asked quickly.

"Well…dat night was serious fi mi. And Limpin – he pay a heavy price. Trojan, Killer, Live Drive. they get off more lightly."

She crouched low beside Grandpa's chair. and rested her hand on his.

"What happened Grandpa?" She said softly. Grandpa sighed.

"Well…" he began. "Dem…dem…" he coughed as he tried to push back the emotion in his voice. "Dem do what we expect from dem kind of people." He said finally. "Tings neva as simple as yu may want fi remember. Dat night, me learn a lot of things. But the main ting mi learn is me learn how fi

121

survive. And dat standing up and being counted…
c'yant be a bad thing. Sandra taught me dat. What it
was she use fi say? United We Stand."

"Sandra?" Kerry-Ann prompted.

"Yes, mi older sister. Yu remember her? She gone
now, same way as Andsurd. But she was always on
dem march dem. Handing out de papers dem." He
kissed his teeth. "Me thought it was useless most
of de time but dat night? Well…it na matter if we
don't win…what matter is we try."

He turned towards Kerry-Ann. "Yu hear?"
He didn't need to say anything else. Kerry-Ann
understood. She nodded.

****

Kerry-Ann's phone buzzed. She looked at the
message.

- *You awake?*
- *Yeah.*
- *U ok?*
- *Nerves, about tomorrow*
- *It'll be ok. I know they're good – but we've got you!*
- *Yeah. No. Dunno. Maybe.*

- *??*

Kerry-Ann paused before typing. How could she put it into words? Everything rested on this moment. She couldn't bear the thought of not getting her last season at the club.

But now Amardeep was typing again.

- *Where does the phrase good innings come from?*

Kerry-Ann smiled.

- *Cricket of course! Used to mean that someone has had a good try at something for a long time.*

- *Did you google it?*

- *No!*

- *Bet u did!*

- *Anyway. Listen, I want to try something new tomorrow. New bat.*

- *You got a new one! What brand?*

- *Not new. Old. Very old! It was my great uncle Andsurd's. And Grandpa's.*

- *Wow.*

- *Yeah. I mean it's family heritage. Might bring me luck, right?*

- *Definitely! Spirit of the ancestors, Kerry-Ann!*

Kerry-Ann laughed out loud. That's why she

loved Amardeep. He always got it.

   - Kind of. And you still ok to captain tomorrow?

   - Sure - anything you want.

   - OK. Good. Night.

CHAPTER FIFTEEN

Kerry-Ann didn't hear Mrs Goody calling "Marnin!" to her as she passed by, head dipped and staring at the ground. She was speed walking to the cricket ground. Bob Marley's '*I shot the Sheriff*' got lost in the white noise of nerves in her head, and the dreadlocked man, a permanent fixture on the wooden bench, didn't even register in her peripheral.

She nearly walked into a man with a bike. The bike was a distraction she didn't need right now… or a memory that she didn't want to think about. She put it from her mind.

Crossing the road, she rounded a bend and approached the cricket ground and, as usual, in her mind she heard the commentary and the roar of the crowd as she entered the gates.

Kerry-Ann Taylor is coming out to bat. The granddaughter of the great Seabert, SeeBee Taylor has a lot riding on this match. Can she do what is required? We will see ladies and gentleman. We will see.

"You're here. Perfect."

Amardeep was waiting to give the team pep-talk. He took Kerry-Ann to the club room where the rest of the side were already waiting. A mix of girls whom she mostly knew, three boys and Amardeep himself of course.

As she followed him she glanced back – the other team was gathering, but there was no sign of Moose.

"Let's talk strategy." Amardeep was saying. "We all know what we are doing, yes?"

Kerry-Ann focused. They had been practising for this. There had only been a few days to prepare, but they knew each other's cricket style, even if they could have done with more time to gel as a team.

"Yes, I know what you're thinking," Amardeep continued. "We haven't had time to grow as a team properly, but we still have a good chance. We have a lot in our armoury. Marcie – you're the best at Yorkers. Don't hold back, use them whenever you see a chance. And Vicki – I've seen your lofted drive

– it's magic."

At the mention of "magic" Amardeep turned his attention to Kerry-Ann. Her face was a mask, fear laced her eyes. He took a deep breath.

"And you, Kerry-Ann Taylor. You are the key to us winning."

She glanced at the bat which lay on top of her bag. That, and Amardeep's words, calmed her nerves.

"You're the perfect all rounder. You've got a killer sweep shot and you can even spin. I don't expect anything less than the best from you."

Kerry-Ann felt the heat rise in her face as her heart swelled with pride.

"This team may be new, but it is strong!"

Kerry-Ann's mouth made a thin, determined line.

"Now," he continued, "let's not forget our strategy."

The white board behind him was marked up with their battle plan.

"We have to target Jack. He's their strongest player. Let's get him out, and get him out fast.

"Danielle?"

Danielle sat up straighter giving Amardeep her full attention. "You are to be our opening bowler." She nodded.

"Try using swing against Jack. If it doesn't work out that's okay, just give it a go. The key is going to be that we are flexible – adapting to the situation as it changes – I'll be making changes as we play and I see how they're responding and what they're thinking. So be ready to switch things up. But most of all – we can do this. I know we can. We just need to give it our best shot.

With the talk over, the team disbanded to collect their thoughts before the match started. Kerry-Ann left the bench and approached Amardeep.

"India versus Pakistan, Virat Kohli?"

Amardeep smiled. "Of course…"

Kerry-Ann grinned back.

Amardeep shrugged. "By the way, your grandparents are here."

CHAPTER SIXTEEN

Kerry-Ann folded her arms. Her eyes narrowed. "What on earth is your problem? Why do you hate me so much?"

Moose was taken aback. He stared at her.

They were standing under the porch at the back of the pavilion. Just the two of them. Kerry-Ann had come out, to get her thoughts together before the game, to get herself centred – she always liked to do that – and found Moose already in her spot.

And right there, the words just came out, surprising her as much as him.

"Well?" she continued, "What have I done to deserve all this? All this hate?"

Moose blinked as if he couldn't believe what she was asking. He turned to go in, to leave the question unanswered, but then stopped.

"You wanna know? Really?"

"Yeah. Go on, whatever you have to say, say it."

"OK. It was your fault. And you never said sorry."

He folded his arms and looked at her, square in the face.

Kerry-Ann froze. He didn't have to say anything more.

She had buried this moment five years ago, or had tried to, but sometimes it still came back to her.

It was night time, the streetlights reflecting on the wet pavement. And she heard that voice again, and the same words, the same worry – the mother, calling to her son.

"Wait for me!"

The boy was running down the path of the front garden, laughing, his blond hair flashing under the winter street lamp, into the dark. The woman, struggling with shopping bags, called after him, louder now.

Then she dumped down her bags, and hurried out onto the pavement.

Kerry-Ann didn't want to remember any more. But she couldn't stop the image coming back – and she couldn't change the past. She saw the woman step out right in front of her. And she was eight again, speeding down the path on her bike – no headlights, brakes not working.

She was late. She was pedalling hard. Mum had specifically told her that she couldn't stay out, but she'd wanted to finish the game at her friend's house. So Mum would be worried. But if she pedalled hard enough, maybe she could get home before Mum did – maybe she could avoid getting into trouble.

After she crashed, after she knocked the woman sideways and flipped over her own handlebars, Kerry-Ann lay stunned for a moment. Her hands were stinging, her knee grazed, nothing more. She picked up her bike.

But the woman wasn't getting up – she was holding her side, groaning with pain.

"Mum! Mum!"

The boy was running back. Kerry-Ann didn't wait. She scrambled onto the saddle, and pedalled. She had to get away.

Now, Moose was still looking at her, arms still folded.

"You always act so innocent. Like you could never do anything wrong. But I was there – I saw you Kerry-Ann. And you never stopped to see if my mum was OK. You've never asked. Not once."

"I…" Kerry-Ann's heart was racing. "I was young, I was scared."

"Yeah me too. I didn't know what to do."

His face was red, his eyes shining.

She reached out, touching his sleeve. And she felt sudden tears prickling her eyes.

"Moose I'm sorry. I was wrong. I should have been better. I should have checked if your mum was OK."

He looked at her.

"I know. But thanks."

Gently, he pushed her hand away.

"Come on. Let's just get this game over with."

He turned to go back in. She reached out again.

"Moose. I'm sorry I did that. I really mean it."

He turned back to her, searching her face.

Then he nodded.

"OK."

CHAPTER SEVENTEEN

In the end, the game came down to the last three balls – three chances for Kerry-Ann's team to reach a winning 186 runs, three chances for Moose's team to stop them – to bowl them out, catch them out, to just close-in and stop them taking the game.

Kerry-Ann's team were on 174 – just 12 short – which meant they needed a minimum four runs from each of the last balls. It was a big ask, but perfectly possible. Just three strong hits, that's all they needed to win.

And finally it came down to the two of them: Kerry-Ann was batting, partnering with Kay, while Moose was lining up to bowl.

Afterwards, it seemed to Kerry-Ann that when the end came a total hush settled over the ground, that everyone who'd gathered to watch – friends from both teams — was suddenly holding their breath. But that silence may just have been in her own mind, as she focused her senses so completely on Moose, and the ball, and the fielders who were leaning in ready to deal with whatever stroke she tried to play.

She had cleared the conversation with Moose from her head – for now – and she felt lighter. She'd been right to apologise. Maybe Moose would never forgive her. Maybe there was no way to earn forgiveness – not like Grandpa running errands after he killed the goat. What errands could Kerry-Ann run?

But she had said she was sorry, and meant it. What happened next, she'd worry about later. For now, the cricket was everything.

And right now she knew it was everything for Moose too. In that, at least, they were agreed.

His first ball was fast, and shot towards the stumps. A good length delivery, it bounced and rose up before her. But Kerry-Ann had judged it well – and it gave her the chance she needed. With all of her weight on her back foot she brought her bat round to meet the rising ball. Her heart leapt as it sailed towards the boundary, landing just over the line. Not a four, but a six.

Not need to run. She'd take the next ball too. Six needed to win, just three runs per ball.

Kerry-Ann readied herself, her confidence lifted by the applause reaching her from her teammates, but not turning to acknowledge them, not yet. She needed to keep focused on Moose as he walked away, turned, and began his second run-up.

Again, Moose bowled fast. And again, Kerry-Ann went for a pull. This time though, the bat clipped it with its top edge – saving the wicket, but presenting an easy catch for Jack. He lunged, blocked it with his fingertips, but couldn't hold it.

Kerry-Ann ignored the gasps, the clapping – Jack returning the ball and saying "come on Moose" – and she refocused.

No runs. Six needed on the last ball. Six to win. It could still be done, and doing it this way would be beautiful. The perfect end to the feud.

Moose must be feeling that too, she thought, as she watched him walk back and turn. He wanted this as much as she did – almost.

But she knew that she wanted it more.

Everything had been leading her to this moment.

She looked down at her bat – Grandpa's bat – and wrapped her right-hand fingers tighter. It felt perfect in her hands.

She was ready.

Moose was sprinting now. Kerry-Ann adjusted her grip on the bat and in her mind's eye she saw her Grandpa playing with his friends in the park. Just having fun. Just enjoying the game. Just loving cricket.

The ball flew out of Moose's hand, hard and fast.

As it sped towards her, she lifted Grandpa's bat. The ball bounced up – but then it spun, curved, shot beneath the bat and smashed into the wicket.

Kerry-Ann heard the cheers and the groans, the boys and the girls living the battle as much as the players on the field. She heard them, as if from a far distance.

The bat hung loosely in her hand.

She'd lost.

CHAPTER EIGHTEEN

Kerry-Ann was in the pavilion, surrounded by friends, but only half in the conversation. They'd lost, yes, but they were happy. She could hear in their voices that they'd enjoyed the game. And none of them had as much riding on this as she did – for them it wasn't personal.

The only one who really understood what this game meant was Amardeep.

Kay and Amy were laughing, Rina was talking about her sisters – plans to play football at the weekend but she wanted them to try cricket too – Kerry-Ann nodded and tried to smile. She felt a hand on her arm.

"You played really well. You should be proud."

She turned. It was Moose.

"Oh – thanks."

"I mean it. I thought you were going to win. And that last ball – I couldn't believe my luck."

He looked at her, and she saw something in his face that she didn't expect – respect? – and she knew that he meant it.

"You won though, right? And I really hoped I was going to."

"But you could have done. It could have gone either way. Next time, eh?" he put out his hand for her to shake.

She took it.

"I've talked to the others," he said. "Told them no arguing, the bet's off. You guys have as much right to play here as we do."

He nodded.

"The club is better with all of us, right? This is your place as much as ours. I get it. Sorry about that stuff before."

She smiled.

Amardeep had appeared.

Moose held out a hand to him too.

"Captain. Your team did good – nice play, really."

"Thanks man, I thought so too."

"Let's make this a regular?" asked Moose. "I was

telling Kerry-Ann – bet's off, right? We can work the rota out so we all play?"

Amardeep glanced at Kerry-Ann.

"Yeah, that's good."

But Kerry-Ann wouldn't be able to play – not next season – there were no mixed teams for anyone over 13.

Club rules. You might win a game, but you could never beat the rules, however well you played, however much you practised.

Kerry-Ann was looking past them, looking towards the door.

Suddenly, all her attention was focused on the figure there – who'd been standing there all along, watching the game – the old man smiling at her, nodding encouragement.

She grinned, and mouthed, "Hey Grandpa."

Grandpa smiled again and nodded – and Kerry-Ann suddenly understood something.

He'd beaten the rules, hadn't he? Bigger rules than a cricket club's.

He'd travelled halfway round the world when

he wasn't much older than she was, he'd come to a strange, cold country that wasn't always welcoming, and he'd fought to build a new life for his friends and family. And when it was hard, he didn't stop trying.

And when the rules weren't fair, he fought to get them changed.

And all through it, he'd kept loving cricket – and cricket had kept loving him.

"Sorry, guys – someone I need to talk to. Back in a minute."

And she was gone. Moose and Amardeep watched as Kerry-Ann headed across the room, not to the door where her grandpa was waiting for her, but to the stairs.

A minute ago Mr Warren had headed up to his office with Mr Finch – the club president and club secretary together. Just the two people who Kerry-Ann needed to talk to.

Why hadn't she thought of this before? The rules said there were no senior teams for girls. Not the right changing facilities, they said. Not enough to make up a team, they said. But the rules needed to be changed. It was possible, if the effort was put in.

And it was Kerry-Ann who was going to make that happen.

It might take her a while to convince them, but she'd keep asking – she'd keep fighting – until they agreed.

She reached the office door at the top of the stairs, raised her fist, and knocked.

CHAPTER NINETEEN

Kerry-Ann and Grandpa came home together, talking all the way about the game.

Nana was in the kitchen cooking up some chicken, coconut rice and peas and Mum was there too, leaning up, drinking tea, chatting to Nana while she cooked. Kerry-Ann's dad was relaxing in the armchair, legs out, feet crossed – he looked up and smiled when they came in.

Grandpa leaned the bat against the fireplace and winked at Kerry-Ann.

"Time to celebrate."

He went over to his record player. He took out an inky-black disc, and placed it on the spinning table. The record turned, the needle bobbing. The sound crackled and popped before music burst out of the speakers. An unmistakable bass guitar playing that signature reggae beat, filled the room.

Nana came to stand in the door.

"Is what dis?"

Grandpa smiled at her, his gold tooth sparkling, and turned the volume up. Janet Kay's voice burst through the speakers, filling the little house.

Grandpa's hand was round Nana's waist now, Mum looked at Kerry-Ann. Kerry-Ann looked at Dad and they all stifled their laughter.

Grandpa was holding Nana's hand so delicately, while Nana was holding up Grandpa. Both of them were grinning.

Then the record ended, and the old couple collapsed laughing.

There was a sudden clattering sound as Dad tipped the box of dominoes out across the table.

"Now's my chance," he said. "You've worn yourselves out – I can beat you now!"

He clapped down his hand, and made the dominoes jump.

"You can try," laughed Grandad. "You can try! But mi not done yet!"

And everyone laughed again, as they gathered round to play. Kerry-Ann clapped her hands. She loved dominoes.

"I'm gonna beat both of you!"

Nana put the record on again – and this time the voice of Janet Kay and the crackles of the record on the smooth black disc mixed with the sounds of laughter, and the noise of the game.

And all of those sounds – the whoops of laughter, the rattle of the pieces, the warmth of the music – burst out of the terraced house window, and danced down the grey London streets.

Cheryl Diane Parkinson
is a British Caribbean author
who writes for adults and
children. Cheryl lives in
Norfolk. She has taught
for 17 years, imparting
her love of English
literature to GCSE and
A Level students. As a writer she enjoys creating
compellng characters, and she is concerned with the
representation of Black people, and equality for all.

Imogyn Nicholas
is an illustrator and character
designer based in Bury St
Edmunds. Originally from
East London, Imogyn
was greatly inspired by the
video games and anime
she watched as a child. Her

bright and colourful illustrations pull heavily from
her background as a second generation British-
Caribbean woman growing up in London.